THE Fairies' Ring
A Book of Fairy Stories & Poems

collected and adapted by **JANE YOLEN**
illustrated by **STEPHEN MACKEY**

MAGIC AHEAD!

DUTTON CHILDREN'S BOOKS • NEW YORK

To my three granddaughters, all of whom love fairies:
Lexi Callan, Maddison Jane Piatt, and Alison Isabelle Stemple

— J. Y.

For William

— S. M.

ACKNOWLEDGMENTS

Page 6, "I'd Love to Be a Fairy's Child." From *Complete Poems: Volume I* by Robert Graves, no date. Reprinted by permission of Carcanet Press Limited.

Page 18, "Fairies." From *Fairies and Chimneys* by Rose Fyleman. Copyright © 1918, 1920 by George H. Doran Company. Used by permission of Doubleday, a division of Random House, Inc., and by permission of the Society of Authors as the literary representative of the Estate of Rose Fyleman.

Page 42, "The Stolen Child," by W. B. Yeats. Reprinted with the permission of Simon & Schuster from *The Poems of W. B. Yeats: A New Edition*, edited by Richard J. Finneran. Copyright © 1983 by Anne Yeats and by permission of A. P. Watt Ltd. on behalf of Michael B. Yeats.

Page 67, "The Stolen Wife." From *Pacific Mythology* by Jan Knappert. Copyright © 1995 by Jan Knappert. Reprinted by permission of HarperCollins Publishers Ltd.

Page 87, "The Ruin," by Walter de la Mare. From *Rhymes and Verses: Collected Poems for Children* by Walter de la Mare. Copyright © 1947 by Henry Holt and Company, Inc. Reprinted by permission of the Literary Trustees of Walter de la Mare and the Society of Authors as their representative.

Library of Congress Cataloging-in-Publication Data
Yolen, Jane.
The fairies' ring: a book of fairy stories & poems / collected and adapted by Jane Yolen;
illustrated by Stephen Mackey.—1st ed.
p. cm.
Summary: A collection of poems by such writers as Robert Graves, William Shakespeare,
and Walter de la Mare and tales from around the world about fairies in all their forms.
ISBN 0-525-46045-4 (hc)
1. Fairies—Literary collections. [1. Fairies—Literary collections.]
I. Mackey, Stephen.   II. Title.
PZ5.Y5Fai   1999   808.8'0375—dc21   99-32230   CIP   AC

Published in the United States by Dutton Children's Books,
a division of Penguin Putnam Books for Young Readers
345 Hudson Street, New York, New York 10014
http://www.penguinputnam.com/yreaders/index.htm
Designed by Sara Reynolds and Richard Amari
Printed in Hong Kong
First Edition
1 3 5 7 9 10 8 6 4 2

Contents

Introduction

Are fairies real?

 No. If you are a scientist who needs proof beyond faith, beyond anecdote, beyond mouth-to-ear resuscitation, there are no fairies. If you are modern, if you are an adult, if you cannot remember childhood, if you need irrefutable facts, there are no fairies.

 Yes. If you are from the nineteenth century or earlier; if you are a storyteller, a peasant nurse, a grandmother, a flower lover, a child, then there are fairies.

Where do fairies come from?

 From the land of the ever-living, a place where there is neither death nor sin, no transgression, or so says the Irish *Book of the Dun Cow*.

 J. M. Barrie, author of *Peter Pan*, says, "When the first baby laughed for the first time, the laugh broke into a thousand pieces, and they all went skipping about and that was the beginning of fairies."

 From the Celtic countries—Ireland, Scotland, England, Wales, Brittany—as well as places like Persia (Iran), New Zealand, South Africa, and Greece. They have flown to far-off lands on wings of story; they have traveled on the backs of storytellers, of sailors and soldiers and slaves.

 Under the floorboards, under a toadstool, under the green hill.

 From our human imagination.

What do fairies look like?

✐ Little winged creatures, very beautiful, very enchanting.

✐ Little winged creatures, very beautiful as long as the glamour is on them, but really they are wizened, thin, ugly, and very, very old.

✐ They come in all shapes and sizes, like the Irish *banshee,* who is a regular-size lady with long, streaming hair and fiery red eyes. Like the English *barguest,* a shape changer who is usually seen as a large black dog with horns and a long tail. Like the *leprechaun,* who is a small man dressed in green. Like the *brownie,* a little hairy man. Like a *changeling,* a piece of rough wood left in a baby's cradle that looks like an ugly version of the child. Like a *knocker,* a little bent-over man who works in Cornish mines but out of sight of the human miners. Like *pigsies,* who are little, pale, slim, and wear no clothes at all.

Are fairies good or bad?

✐ Yes.

✐ Some fairies are good. They sweep the house, they leave presents, they help with child care.

✐ Some fairies are bad. They steal babies, they blind old midwives, they take folk to fairyland for a hundred years.

✐ We have no way of guessing which fairy will be good or which will be bad. They are amoral, which means they have no morals at all, either good or bad. They are just…fairies. So one must always be careful in dealing with them.

Do you believe in fairies?

✐ Yes, when I am reading their stories. When I am writing about them. When I am choosing my favorites for this book.

✐ No, when I am being brutally and flat-footedly honest.

✐ I have never seen a fairy.

JANE YOLEN, *Phoenix Farm*

I'd Love to Be a Fairy's Child

Children born of fairy stock
Never need for shirt or frock,
Never want for food or fire,
Always get their heart's desire:
Jingle pockets full of gold,
Marry when they're seven years old.
Every fairy child may keep
Two strong ponies and ten sheep;
All have houses, each his own,
Built of brick or granite stone;
They live on cherries, they run wild—
I'd love to be a fairy's child.

ROBERT GRAVES

Thomas the Rhymer

SCOTLAND

OUNG THOMAS OF ERCILDOUNE walked out one May morning along Huntlie Burn, that lovely stream that rushes down the slopes of the Eildon Hills. He had come a long way and lay down to rest on the greening banks.

As he lay there, half dreaming, he heard the sound of horse's hooves and the tinkling of what sounded like a hundred tiny bells.

Sitting up, he spied a beautiful lady riding toward him on a fine horse. She wore a hunting dress of glistening grass-green silk and a velvet mantle of the same hue. On her head was a diadem of precious stones. On every tuft of her horse's mane was hung a silver bell.

Thomas leaped up and snatched off his cap, then fell to one knee. "Hail to thee, queen of Heaven," he cried, "for thy peer on Earth I have never seen."

The lady threw back her head and laughed, and her laugh was even lovelier than bells. "I am neither queen on Earth or in Heaven. I am the queen of fair Elfland, come to visit here for a while."

Thomas all but fell in a swoon before her. "Pray give me a kiss, lady, or I will die." He said it knowing the power of the fairy queen, but he was already in her thrall.

"A kiss you shall have, Thomas," she replied.

And then she kissed him on the lips.

At the very meeting of their lips, he felt such sweetness, he almost fainted, but when he opened his eyes, he no longer saw the beautiful queen before him. In her place was an old hag, her face a mass of deep wrinkles and her silken gown a gray rag.

"Am I no longer fair, my Thomas?" asked the queen.

He could not speak, neither yea nor nay.

She smiled, and the smile did not go all the way to her eyes. "It does not matter, my lad, for with that kiss you are mine for seven years."

"Mercy," Thomas said, a small word for such a big request.

"No, no mercy, Thomas. You asked for the kiss without asking the price. Now you must pay its worth without complaint. Seven full years you must dwell with me. So mount up behind."

He could not disobey. So with many a sigh and groan of terror, he got up behind her and away they went, leaving the land of the living behind.

THEY RODE ON and on and on, coming at last to a broad desert where three roads lay before them. One was broad and level, and it ran straight across the sand. One was narrow and winding with a thorn on one side and a briar on the other. The third was a bonnie road, winding easily among the bracken and heather.

"Which road would you choose, my Thomas?" asked the queen. But before he could reply, she added: "That broad road is the way to Hell, and the narrow one the way to Heaven. But the third road is the way to Elfland where you and I must go."

Sitting behind the queen, Thomas shivered, though he was not cold.

"One warning I will give you, Thomas, before we get to my kingdom."

"I hear, my lady," he whispered from behind her.

"If you ever hope to see your home in Ercildoune again, you must guard your tongue. Do not speak a single word in Elfland to anyone but me. For the mortal who opens his lips rashly in Elfland must bide there forever and a day."

"I hear, my lady," said Thomas, "and I obey."

SO OFF THEY TROTTED along the bonnie road, but it was not bonnie for very long. Soon the way became tangled and dark. The air felt heavy and dank. They crossed a river of blood, red and cold, and Thomas might have fallen off and drowned but that he had his arms round about the old hag's waist.

And in this way they rode through darkness into light and came at last to an orchard filled with fruit trees: pears and peaches and figs and dates.

"Stop, mistress, I beg you, and let me have something to eat, for I have not had a bite this whole day."

The queen would not stop, saying only, "There is nothing here that you can eat, save an apple I shall give you a little ways on, for if you have a bite of anything but that which I give to you, you will remain in Elfland forever."

So they rode on and on till they came at last to a small tree on which grew seven red apples. The fairy queen reached up and plucked one. She gave it to him, saying, "These apples are the Apples of Truth, and once you have eaten but a single bite, you will never again be able to tell a lie."

Thomas ate the apple, pips and all, for he was that hungry.

As soon as he was done, he saw that they were in Elfland proper, and suddenly they were surrounded by all manner of strange folk: sprites and fairies, pixies and elves, men with antlers and ladies with hooves, swan maidens and seal maidens, and fiddlers and fools.

The fairy queen blew upon a hunting horn that hung at her side. At the sound of the blast, she changed back into the beautiful lady, young and handsome, in grass-green silk.

And lo! Thomas was transformed as well, his rough country clothes now a silken suit, and on his feet satin shoes.

"This is True Thomas," the queen said to the Elfland folk who assembled before her. "He cannot speak. Nor will he for the seven years he lives among us."

And so it was. One day and the next and the next.

Thomas was astonished at everything he saw: the fairy ladies with their wings, the pixie men with their red caps, the nuggles and the boggles and the fairy fiddlers who played tunes that made the heart to sing and the feet to dance.

Three days and three nights he was at the fairy court and did not say a word.

At the end of that time, the fairy queen came to him and said, "You must mount behind me and ride, True Thomas, if you would ever see your home again."

He shook his head in amazement. "But I have been here only three days."

The fairy queen smiled. "Time passes strangely for mortals in fairyland. Though it has been but three days here, it has been seven years on the Earth. I would have you stay longer, but for your own sake, True Thomas, you must go. Every seven years we here in Elfland must pay a tithe to Hell. The Devil himself comes to pick one soul, and as you are such a goodly fellow, I fear it might be you."

So up behind her Thomas mounted again, and they passed across the river of blood and through the darkness to the light, arriving at last at where the three roads came together.

There the queen turned and said, "Thomas, I have given you the gift of Truth, but I shall give you the gift of Prophecy as well, for you were a fine servant for seven years and did not once speak. And because humans do not believe what they cannot see, I will give you a fairy harp as well, so you can make the sweetest music ever heard by man."

"But I cannot play," Thomas said.

"The harp will teach you how," she answered. Then she bade him dismount and before he could say good-bye, she was gone on the bonnie road and out of sight.

· · ·

THOMAS OF ERCILDOUNE found his way back home, and his friends and family were surprised to see him alive, for he had been gone seven long years, and they thought him dead for sure. Indeed no one but his old dog recognized him at first, for Thomas was gaunt and wild-eyed, and his beard had grown down to his belt.

But at last shaven and shorn, he was welcomed home where, with his gift for the truth, they called him True Thomas. And because of his gift for poetic prophecies that always came true, they called him Thomas the Rhymer as well.

He married a local girl and raised a family, and in time—when his father died—he became the Laird of Ercildoune.

So for fourteen years—which he thought must be but six days in Faerie—Thomas spoke truly and played his fairy harp. He was a generous laird, good to his tenants, and fair.

Then one evening he gave a great feast for all the Scottish armies that were resting by the banks of the Tweed, not far from his home.

That night after the feast, a soldier on guard in the encampment saw a snow-white hart and hind going slowly along the road between their camp and Thomas's tower home.

The captain sent a message to Ercildoune asking if True Thomas could tell them the meaning of such a wonder. Would they win their battle or lose it?

Thomas was in bed when the messenger came, but he sat up at once. "It is a summons from the queen of Elfland," he said. "It has come at last."

He arose, got dressed, and followed the boy back to camp. But instead of speaking to the captain or his men, Thomas went straight up to the white deer. The deer paused for a moment, nodding as if greeting him. Then the three of them disappeared down an embankment and were gone from sight.

The soldiers searched through the night and into the dawn, but Thomas of Ercildoune was never seen again. The folks who knew said that he had gone back along the bonnie road to Elfland where his heart had ever been, leaving wife and family and Ercildoune far behind. 🌿

The Queen of the Fay

Four and forty are the braids
That twine about her head.
Four and forty are the maids
That wait upon her bed.
Four and forty are the bells
Upon her horse's bridle,
Four and forty are the jewels
Upon its leather saddle.
Four and forty are the babes
That she has stole away,
And countless are the princes' hearts
That she did break today.

JANE YOLEN

Fairies

There are fairies at the bottom of our garden!
    It's not so very, very far away;
You pass the gardener's shed and you just keep straight ahead—
    I do so hope they've really come to stay.
There's a little wood, with moss in it and beetles,
    And a little stream that quietly runs through;
You wouldn't think they'd dare to come merrymaking there—
    Well, they do.

There are fairies at the bottom of our garden!
    They often have a dance on summer nights;
The butterflies and bees make a lovely little breeze,
    And the rabbits stand about and hold the lights.
Did you know that they could sit upon the moonbeams
    And pick a little star to make a fan,
And dance away up there in the middle of the air?
    Well, they can.

There are fairies at the bottom of our garden!
    You cannot think how beautiful they are;
They all stand up and sing when the Fairy Queen and King
    Come gently floating down upon their car.
The King is very proud and *very* handsome;
    The Queen—now can you guess who that could be?
(She's a little girl all day, but at night she steals away.)
    Well—it's *me*!

ROSE FYLEMAN

The Peri Wife

NCE THERE WAS AND THERE WAS NOT a merchant in the city of Hindustan who had an only son named Ali. But so wild and undutiful a boy was he, that at last his despairing father drove him away.

Dressed in the clothes of a wandering dervish, Ali left his father's house and walked for many miles. But overcome with fatigue, he left the high road and sat down to rest in a small grove of trees by a little pool.

It was just sunset; four white doves flew down from one of the trees in the grove, and when they reached the ground, they changed into four of the most beautiful young women Ali had ever seen.

The sun, the moon have never so perfect a form, Ali thought. He knew at once they were Peries, those magnificent fairies who lived on the smell of perfume.

They stripped off their white shifts and went into the pool where they splashed one another and laughed in lovely voices that sounded like birds singing.

While they were playing, Ali stood up quietly and crept to where their garments had been left upon the sand. He gathered these up and crept back to the grove, where he placed the clothing in the hollow of one of the trees. Then he hid behind that very tree.

When the Peries came out of the water and could not find their shifts, they were distressed beyond measure. They ran about this way and that, looking for their clothes, but all in vain.

One of them—the youngest and handsomest—spied Ali, and, guessing immediately that he had taken their shifts, she alerted her sisters. Then she came over to him and cried.

"Please, son of Adam, return us our shifts, for without them we cannot change form."

"Only if you consent to be my wife," said Ali.

"But marriage between us is impossible," the Peri said. "For I am made of fire, and you of earth and water."

"Nevertheless," Ali insisted, "your sisters shall not have the return of their shifts unless you promise to be my bride."

At last the Peri saw that her pleadings were useless. She bid her sisters a tearful farewell. Then Ali gave them back their shifts, all but his Peri wife. The other fairy maidens turned into doves and flew off, but the Peri wife remained behind.

ALI RETURNED HOME with his lovely bride and was forgiven at once, for his father thought that with so beautiful and docile a wife, his son would soon mend his ways.

For a long time this was true. Ali stayed comfortably at home, making certain that his bride was clothed in the most costly raiment and draped in jewels. But her Peri shift he buried in a secret place in the far end of the walled garden, for he did not want her ever to leave.

The Peri had been wrong about the sons of Adam wedding fairy wives. Fire and earth and water produced three handsome sons and three lovely daughters whom she loved. She learned to take some pleasure in the company of her husband's friends and relatives. Ali was sure of her affection, and so he took no other wife.

But when Ali's father died, it soon became known that the old man had not been a wise and careful merchant. There was little enough money left after he was buried, and so Ali was forced to go off on a long voyage to try to regain the family's fortune.

He put his wife and home in the charge of an old woman who had served the family for years.

Taking the old woman aside, he said, "You already know my wife is a Peri. But should anything happen to me and I not return, someone should know my greatest secret: Her Peri shift lies buried in the far corner of the garden." And he showed the old woman where.

Then off he sailed.

THE OLD WOMAN was sad, and so were his children, that Ali had gone without them. But the Peri wife seemed saddest of all, for she wept continuously and would not be comforted.

It was not three days later that, having just bathed, the Peri wife was drying her amber-scented hair with the corner of her veil. The old woman was helping her, and she murmured over and over about the Peri's great beauty.

"Ah, nurse," the Peri replied, "I am no beauty now. If you could see me for just one moment in my Peri shift, then you would know why the poets sing that: *The sun, the moon have never so perfect a form.*"

The nurse said, "I cannot believe you could be any more beautiful, my lady."

The Peri smiled sadly. "It is said that we are the most finished portrait on the tablets of existence. What you see now is but a sketch for that portrait. Ah, had I my Peri shift, you should see me as I should be seen."

"I know where your shift is, my lady," said the old woman.

The Peri smiled a smile of such sweetness, it seemed a lamp had been lit in the room. "Then let me put it on for a single moment, dear nurse—one moment only—and I will show you my native beauty, the likes of which only my lord husband has gazed upon."

The silly old woman went at once and dug up the Peri's shift which, though it had been in dirt all those years, still gleamed perfectly white. She brought it to her mistress.

"Watch closely, dear nurse," the Peri wife said, and put on the shift. No sooner had it slipped down over her head than she turned into a dove and escaped—crying her freedom in a thrilled voice—into the darkling air.

WHEN THE MERCHANT returned from his successful voyage and found his wife gone, he became possessed, weeping and crying and calling out day and night.

Peri-stricken, it is called. And thus he remained, confined in a madman's cell to the end of his life. ✒

Catching Fairies

They're sleeping beneath the roses;
  Oh! kiss them before they rise,
And tickle their tiny noses,
  And sprinkle the dew on their eyes.
    Make haste, make haste;
    The faires are caught;
    Make haste.

We'll put them in silver cages,
  And send them full-dress'd to court,
And maids of honor and pages
  Shall turn the poor things to sport.
    Be quick, be quick;
    Be quicker than thought;
    Be quick.

Their scarves shall be pennons for lancers,
  We'll tie up our flowers with their curls,
Their plumes will make fans for dancers,
  Their tears shall be set with pearls.
    Be wise, be wise;
    Make the most of the prize;
    Be wise.

They'll scatter sweet scents by winking,
  With sparks from under their feet;
They'll save us the trouble of thinking,
  Their voices will sound so sweet.
    Oh stay, oh stay:
    They're up and away:
    Oh stay!

WILLIAM CORY

The Fairy Midwife

ENGLAND

NCE IN THE TOWN of Nether Witton there lived a midwife named Maggie Brown who was known far and wide for her skills. She had hands like clouds, and a heart full of healing, or so it was said the countryside around.

One night, when the moon was gone behind shreds of clouds, a messenger came to her door.

"My master's wife is in childbed, but the child will not come."

"Do I have your master's name?" asked Maggie.

"Ye shall have neither his name nor his dwelling," said the messenger, "for ye must be carried there blindfolded, and back as well."

Maggie did not know the messenger, nor did she like his manner, but when he showed her the size of the purse and the number of coins she was to have for her work, she consented.

He blindfolded her and set her up on a great steed. Then he climbed on behind. And off they went, the wind blowing hard against them, the horse so fine an animal that she felt neither ground nor gravel beneath its feet.

The journey was short, and when Maggie was helped down and the bandage removed from her eyes, she saw that she was in a big room. There were tapestries on the wall and rushes on the floor, a cozy fire in the hearth and metalwork lanterns shedding light.

On a great bed that was hung with embroidered draperies lay the master's wife, and she was laboring hard but to no avail.

"There, there, my dove; there, there, my hinny," said Maggie, for she always spoke to the women that way till after they gave birth, and then it was "my mistress," and "my lady."

The woman looked up groggily, saw Maggie, and relaxed. So Maggie rolled up her sleeves and went to work. Within minutes the baby was safely born.

Maggie wrapped the child—a little girl it was—in swaddling and was about to place her in her mother's arms when an old nurse who had been standing by handed Maggie a box of ointment.

"Rub the child all over with this," said the old woman. "It is the custom of the house. But be careful ye do not get it in yer eye, for it will go ill with ye."

So Maggie unwrapped the babe and rubbed it well with the ointment as instructed. But as she was working, she felt an overwhelming itching in her left eye and, without thinking, she rubbed it with the very finger that had ointment on it.

At that same moment, all that she saw with that eye changed. No longer was she in a room of a grand house, hung about with tapestries. Instead she saw truly that she was in a fairy mound. The cozy fire was the hollowed trunk of an old oak. Glowworms were what she had mistaken for tapers, moss for tapestries. The bed was a pile of straw hung about with dead leaves. The lady in the straw was a fairy whose gauze wings were a bit tattered and torn.

Maggie did not show her amazement for fear of being found out. Instead she simply wrapped the baby back up in its swaddlings and handed it to the fairy mother in the bed, saying: "Your child, my lady, and may you have good fortune of her."

Then the messenger covered up her eyes again, threw her up atop the great horse, and away they rode, over broom and briar but never touching the ground.

THE FAIRY COIN Maggie was given for her work proved true. And all should have been well. But a few weeks later, on a marketing day, Maggie chanced to see the old fairy nurse wandering among the countrywomen at the fair. She was gliding about and taking this from one basket, that from another, passing a little wooden scraper along the rolls of butter, and dipping a little wooden ladle in the milk jugs with no one the wiser.

Without thinking of the consequences, Maggie nodded at the old woman as one would to an acquaintance.

The old woman nodded back. "And which eye, Maggie Brown, do ye see me with?"

"Why, this one," Maggie innocently replied, pointing to the left eye.

The fairy nurse leaned over and blew on the eye, and the cold breath clouded it over forever. Then the fairy vanished, and Maggie was left, one-sighted and forlorn, at the fair. ✍

The Fairies

Up the airy mountain,
    Down the rushy glen,
We daren't go a-hunting
    For fear of little men;
Wee folk, good folk,
    Trooping all together;
Green jacket, red cap,
    And white owl's feather!

Down along the rocky shore
    Some make their home,
They live on crispy pancakes
    Of yellow tide-foam;
Some in the reeds
    Of the black mountain lake,
With frogs for their watch-dogs,
    All night awake.

High on the hill-top
    The old King sits;
He is now so old and gray
    He's nigh lost his wits.
With a bridge of white mist
    Columbkill he crosses,
On his stately journeys
    From Slieveleague to Rosses;
Or going up with music
    On cold starry nights,
To sup with the Queen
    Of the gay Northern Lights.

They stole little Bridget
    For seven years long;
When she came down again
    Her friends were all gone.
They took her lightly back,
    Between the night and morrow,
They thought that she was fast asleep,
    But she was dead with sorrow.
They have kept her ever since
    Deep within the lake,
On a bed of flag-leaves,
    Watching till she wake.

By the craggy hill-side,
    Through the mosses bare,
They have planted thorn-trees
    For pleasure here and there.
Is any man so daring
    As dig them up in spite,
He shall find their sharpest thorns
    In his bed at night.

Up the airy mountain,
    Down the rushy glen,
We daren't go a-hunting
    For fear of little men;
Wee folk, good folk,
    Trooping all together;
Green jacket, red cap,
    And white owl's feather!

WILLIAM ALLINGHAM

The Fee's Changeling

FRANCE — NORMANDY

 **I**N NORMANDY on a brilliant summer day, a woman was carrying her one-month-old baby back from visiting her mother. Along the road, she came upon a fairy woman—a Fee—who was as beautiful as a new moon, and who held a child of the same age in her arms.

As new mothers will, they chatted and exclaimed about one another's infants, though the human woman saw that the Fee's child was nine times finer than her own. She said as much to the Fee.

"Will you exchange them then?" asked the Fee, holding her baby out.

"Oh, Madame Fee," said the woman, "though your child be more beautiful than the moon and more glorious than the sun, still I will not change it for my own." And she clutched her baby to her breast and went immediately home.

A FEW DAYS LATER, the woman left her child sleeping in the cottage and went outside into her garden to pick some peas. When she returned she saw that the child in the cradle was not her own. It was an ugly, wizened thing, with thinning hair and a permanent sneer.

Weeping and wailing, she cried until her heart almost burst in two. But the curé—the local priest—was walking by and hearing her sobs, came in.

"Ah, my daughter, and you believe a Fee has exchanged her child for yours," said the curé. "But sometimes what looked lovely at first glance seems ugly later on. Are you certain?"

"I am the mother," said the woman. "Of course I am certain."

"First I shall need proof," said the curé, and he broke a dozen eggs and ranged the shells before the child.

The child sat up in the cradle—something no month-old child can do—and cried out, "Oh! What a number of cream pots. Oh! What a number of cream pots!"

"Aha," said the curé. "A changeling indeed."

"Now what to do?" asked the woman, who had never been in doubt that the child in the cradle was not hers.

"Take it to the marketplace," advised the curé, "and make it scream lustily."

So the woman did this at once, and in the marketplace she set about berating the changeling, pinching it and shouting at it till it began to cry loud and long.

At once the Fee appeared with woman's own child in her arms.

"Stop, stop, do not hurt my baby," said the Fee. "Take yours back, and we will be quits."

Hastily, the woman took her own child back and, the exchange being made, ran gratefully home.

She was never bothered by the Fee again. 🍃

The Fairies' Dance

Dare you haunt our hallow'd green?
None but fairies here are seen.
Down and sleep
Wake and weep,
Pinch him black, and pinch him blue,
That seeks to steal a lover true!
When you come to hear us sing,
Or to tread our fairy ring,
Pinch him black, and pinch him blue!
Oh, thus our nails shall handle you!

ANONYMOUS

Queen Mab

This is Mab, the mistress Fairy,
That doth nightly rob the dairy,
And can help or hurt the churning,
As she please without discerning.

She that pinches country wenches,
If they rub not clean their benches,
And with sharper nails remembers
When they rake not up their embers:
But if so they chance to feast her,
In a shoe she drops a tester.

This is she that empties cradles,
Takes out children, puts in ladles:
Trains forth midwives in their slumber,
With a sieve the holes to number;
And then leads them from her burrows,
Home through ponds and water-furrows.

She can start our Franklin's daughters,
In their sleep, with shrieks and laughters;
And on sweet St. Anna's night,
Feed them with a promised sight,
Some of husbands, some of lovers,
Which an empty dream discovers.

BEN JONSON

The Fairies Banished

ONCE IN A SMALL TOWN IN WALES there was a small farmhouse where the kitchen and cowshed were on the very same floor with only a wooden partition between. To this farmhouse a troop of fairies came a-haunting, and no good came from them.

If the family was sitting at a meal in the kitchen, the fairies went a-racketing in the cowshed: flinging straw about, pulling the cows' tails, and generally making a nuisance of themselves.

And if the family was engaged in milking the cows, the fairies were making a riot in the kitchen: getting into the flour and flinging it about, leaving tiny handprints in the butter, and dumping the precious salt onto the floor.

Oh, there was no end to their mischief.

Now one evening, after a long month of this rioting, a parcel of reapers were at their harvest dinner in the kitchen. The fairies started up with the cows, laughing and dancing and throwing quantities of dirt and dust around that—of course—spread over the partition and quite spoiled the meal.

One of the reapers, an old woman who had been traveling for most of her long years, took the mistress of the house aside. "I can provide a remedy for this mischief," she said.

"Oh, please," said the housewife. "For we are out of our minds with it."

So taking aside six of the reapers, the old woman—in the hearing of the fairies—said, "The mistress invites you all to come to dinner again tomorrow."

When they arrived the next evening, the mistress of the house—according to instructions from the old woman—had boiled up a pudding in an eggshell.

The fairies gathered on top of the partition and watched, muttering among themselves. However, the six men acted as if nothing were unusual and ate the eggshell pudding with loud smackings of their lips. For the old woman had told them what parts they were to play.

At length one of the fairies announced: "We have lived long in this world, having been born just after the Earth was made and before the first acorn was planted. Yet we never saw a harvest-dinner pudding made in an eggshell and served to six strong men. There must be something wrong with this house, and we will stay here no longer."

Then away they went and never returned.

As for the old woman, she got to stop her travelings and live comfortably in the farmhouse as a member of the family till the end of her days. ✍

Fairy Song

What I am I must not show—
What I am thou couldst not know—
Something betwixt heaven and hell—
Something that neither stood nor fell—
Something that through thy wit or will
May work thee good—may work thee ill.
Neither substance quite, nor shadow,
Haunting lonely moor and meadow,
Dancing by the haunted spring,
Riding on the whirlwind's wing;
Aping in fantastic fashion
Every change of human passion,
While o'er our frozen minds they pass,
Like shadows from the mirror'd glass.
Wayward, fickle, is our mood,
Hovering betwixt bad and good,
Happier than brief-dated man,
Living ten times o'er his span;
Far less happy, for we have
Help nor hope beyond the grave!

SIR WALTER SCOTT

The Stolen Child

Where dips the rocky highland
Of Sleuth Wood in the lake,
There lies a leafy island
Where flapping herons wake
The drowsy water-rats;
There we've hid our faery vats
Full of berries,
And of reddest stolen cherries.
Come away, O human child!
To the waters and the wild
With a faery, hand in hand,
For the world's more full of weeping than
*   you can understand.*

Where the wave of moonlight glosses
The dim gray sands with light,
Far off by furthest Rosses
We foot it all the night,
Weaving olden dances,
Mingling hands and mingling glances
Till the moon has taken flight;
To and fro we leap
And chase the frothy bubbles,
While the world is full of troubles
And is anxious in its sleep.
Come away, O human child!
To the waters and the wild
With a faery, hand in hand,
For the world's more full of weeping
*   than you can understand.*

Where the wandering water gushes
From the hills above Glen-Car,
In pools among the rushes
That scarce could bathe a star,
We seek for slumbering trout
And whispering in their ears
Give them unquiet dreams;
Leaning softly out
From ferns that drop their tears
Over the young streams,
Come away, O human child!
To the waters and the wild
With a faery, hand in hand,
For the world's more full of weeping
          than you can understand.

Away with us he's going,
The solemn-eyed:
He'll hear no more the lowing
Of the calves on the warm hillside;
Or the kettle on the hob
Sing peace into his breast,
Or see the brown mice bob
Round and round the oatmeal-chest.
For he comes, the human child,
To the waters and the wild
With a faery, hand in hand,
From a world more full of weeping
          than he can understand.

W. B. YEATS

The Faery Flag

LONG AGO, WHEN THE WIND blew from one corner of Skye to another without ever encountering a house higher than a tree, the faery folk lived on the land and they were called the *Daoine Sidhe*, the People of Peace. They loved the land well and shepherded its flock, and never a building did they build that could not be dismantled in a single night or put up again in a single day.

But then human folk set foot upon the isles and scoured them with their rough shoeing. And before long both rock and tree were in the employ of men; the land filled with forts and houses, byres and pens. Boats plowed the seas and netted the fish. Stones were piled up for fences between neighbors.

The *Daoine Sidhe* were not pleased, not pleased at all. An edict went out from the faery chief: *Have nothing to do with this humankind.*

And for year upon year it was so.

Now one day, the young laird of the MacLeod clan—Jamie was his name—walked out beyond his manor seeking a brachet lost outside in the night. It was his favorite hound, as old as he, which—since he was just past fifteen years—was quite old indeed.

He called its name. "Leoid. Leeeeeooid." The wind sent back the name against his face, but the dog never answered.

The day was chill, the wind was cold, and a white mist swirled about the young laird. But many days on Skye are thus, and he thought no more about the chill and cold than that he must find his old hound lest it die.

Jamie paid no heed to where his feet led him, through the bogs and over the hummocks. This was his land, after all, and he knew it well. He could not see the towering crags of the Black Cuillins, though he knew they were there. He could not hear the seals calling from the bay. Leoid was all he cared about. A MacLeod takes care of his own.

So without knowing it, he crossed over a strange, low, stone *drochit*, a bridge the likes of which he would never have found on a sunny day, for it was the bridge into Faerie.

No sooner had he crossed over than he heard his old dog barking. He would have known that sound were there a hundred howling hounds.

"Leoid!" he called. And the dog ran up to him, its hind end wagging, eager as a pup, so happy it was to see him. It had been made young again in the land of Faerie.

Jamie gathered the dog in his arms and was just turning to go when he heard a girl calling from behind him.

"Leoid. Leoid." Her voice was as full of longing as his own had been just moments before.

He turned back, the dog still in his arms, and the fog lifted. Running toward him was the most beautiful girl he had ever seen. Her dark hair was wild with curls, her black eyes wide, her mouth generous and smiling.

"Boy, you have found my dog. Give it to me."

Now that was surely no way to speak to the young laird of the MacLeods, he who would someday be the chief. But the girl did not seem to know him. And surely he did not know the girl, though he knew everyone under his father's rule.

"This is my dog," said Jamie.

The girl came closer and put out her hand. She touched him on his bare arm. Where her hand touched he felt such a shock, he thought he would die, but of love not of fear. Yet he did not.

"It is my dog now, Jamie MacLeod," she said. "It has crossed over the bridge. It has eaten the food of the *Daoine Sidhe* and drunk our honey wine. If you bring it back to your world, it will die at once and crumble into dust."

The young laird set the dog down and it frolicked about his feet. He put his hand into the girl's but was not shocked again.

"I will give it back to you for your name—and a kiss," he said.

"Be warned," answered the girl.

"I know about faery kisses," said Jamie, "but I am not afraid. And as you know my name, it is only fair that I should know yours."

"What we consider fair you do not, young laird," she said. But she stood on tiptoe and kissed him on the brow. "Do not come back across the bridge, or you will break your parents' hearts."

He handed her the sprig of juniper from his bonnet.

She kissed the sprig as well and put it in her hair. "My name is Aizel and, like the red hot cinder, I burn what I touch." Then she whistled for the dog, and they disappeared at once into the mist.

Jamie put his hand to his brow where Aizel had kissed him, and indeed she had burned him. It was still warm and sweet to his touch.

DESPITE THE FAERY girl's warning, Jamie MacLeod looked for the bridge not once but many times. He left off fishing to search for it, and interrupted his hunting to search for it, and often he left his bed when the mist was thick to seek it. But even in the mist and the rain and the fog he could not find it. Yet he never stopped longing for the bridge to the girl. His mother and father grew worried. They guessed by the mark on his brow what had occurred. So they gave great parties and threw magnificent balls that in this way the young laird might meet a human girl and forget the girl of the *Daoine Sidhe*.

But never was there a girl he danced with that he danced with again. Never a girl he held that he held for long. Never a girl he kissed that he did not remember Aizel at the bridge. As time went on, his mother and father grew so desperate for him to give the MacLeods an heir that they would have let him marry any young woman at all, even a faery maid.

ON THE EVE of Jamie's twenty-first birthday, there was a great gathering of the clan at Dunvegan Castle. All the lights were set out along the castle wall, and they twinned themselves down in the bay below.

Jamie walked the ramparts and stared out across the bogs and drums. "Oh, Aizel," he said with a great sigh, "if I could but see you one more time. One more time and I'd be content."

And then he thought he heard the barking of a dog.

Now there were hounds in the castle and hounds in the town and hounds that ran every day under his horse's hooves. But he knew that particular call.

"Leoid!" he whispered to himself. He raced down the stairs and out the great doors with a torch in his hand, following the barking across the bog.

It was a misty, moisty evening, but he seemed to know the way. And he came quite soon to the cobbled bridge that he had so long sought. For a moment, he hesitated, then went on.

There, in the middle, not looking a day older than when he had seen her six years before, stood Aizel in her green gown. Leoid was by her side.

"Into your majority, young laird," said Aizel. "I called to wish you the best."

"It is the best, now that I can see you," Jamie said. He smiled. "And my old dog."

Aizel smiled back. "No older than when last you saw us."

"I have thought of you every day since you kissed me," said Jamie. "And longed for you every night. Your brand still burns on my brow."

"I warned you of faery kisses," said Aizel.

He lifted his bonnet and pushed away his hair to show her the mark.

"I have thought of you, too, young laird," said Aizel. "And how the MacLeods have kept the peace in this unpeaceful land. My chief says I may bide with you for a while."

"How long a while?" asked Jamie.

"A faery while," replied Aizel. "A year or an heir, whichever comes first."

"A year is such a short time," Jamie said.

"I can make it be forever," Aizel answered.

With that riddle, Jamie was content. And they walked back to Dunvegan Castle hand in hand, though they left the dog behind.

If Aizel seemed less fey in the starlight, Jamie did not mind. If he was only human, she did not seem to care. Nothing really mattered but his hand in hers, her hand in his, all the way back to his home.

The chief of the MacLeods was not pleased, and his wife was not happy with the match. But that Jamie smiled and was content made them hold their tongues. So the young laird and the faery maid were married that night and bedded before day.

And in the evening Aizel came to them and said, "The MacLeods shall have their heir."

The days went fast and slow, warm and cold, and longer than a human it took for the faery girl to bear a child. But on the last day of the year she had lived with them, Aizel was brought to labor till with a great happy sigh she birthed a beautiful babe.

"A boy!" the midwife called out, standing on a chair and showing the child so that all the MacLeods might see.

A great cheer ran around the castle then. "An heir. An heir to the MacLeods!"

Jamie was happy for that, but happier still that his faery wife was well. He bent to kiss her brow.

"A year or an heir, that was all I could promise. But I have given you forever," she said. "The MacLeods shall prosper and Dunvegan will never fall."

Before he could say a word in return, she had vanished and the bed was bare, though her outline could be seen on the linens for a moment more.

The cheer was still echoing along the stone passageways as the midwife carried the babe from room to room to show him to all the clan. But the young laird of the MacLeods put his head in his hands and wept.

LATER THAT NIGHT, when the fires were high in every hearth and blaeberry wine filled every cup, when the harp and fiddle rang throughout Dunvegan with their tunes, when the bards' mouths swilled with whisky and swelled with old songs, and when the nurse was dancing with her man, the young laird Jamie MacLeod walked the castle ramparts seven times round, mourning for his lost faery wife.

The youngest laird of the MacLeods lay in his cradle all alone.

So great was the celebration that no one was watching him. And in the deepest part of the night, he kicked off his blankets as babies often do, and he cried out with the cold.

But no one came to cover him. Not the nurse dancing with her man, nor his grandam listening to the tunes, nor his grandfather drinking with his men, nor his father on the castle walk. No one heard the poor wee babe crying with the cold.

It was a tiny cry, a thin bit of sound threaded out into the dark. It went over hillock and hill, over barrow and bog, crossed the cobbled *drochit*, and wound its way into Faerie itself.

Now they were celebrating in the faery world as well, not for the birth of the child but for the return of their own. There was feasting and dancing and singing of tunes. There was honey wine and faery pipes and the high, sweet laughter of the *Daoine Sidhe*.

But in all that fine company, Aizel alone did not sing and dance. She sat in her great chair with her arm around her brachet. If there were tears in her eyes, you would not have known it, for the *Daoine Sidhe* do not cry, and besides the hound had licked away every one. But she heard that tiny sound as any mother would. Distracted, she stood.

"What is it, my daughter?" asked the great chief of the *Daoine Sidhe* when he saw her stand, when he saw a single tear that Leoid had not had time to lick away.

But before any of the fey could tell her no, Aizel ran from the faery hall, the dog at her heels. She raced across the bridge, herself as insubstantial as the mist. And behind her came the faery troops. And the dog.

The company of fey stopped at the edge of the bridge and watched Aizel go. Leoid followed right after. But no sooner had the dog's legs touched the earth on the other side than it crumbled into dust.

Aizel hesitated not a moment but followed the thread of sound, winding her back into the world of men. She walked over bog and barrow, over hill and hillock, through the great wooden doors and up the castle stairs.

When she entered the baby's room, he was between one breath and another.

"There, there," Aizel said, leaning over the cradle and covering him with her shawl, "thy mama's here." She rocked him till he fell back asleep, warm and content. Then she kissed him on the brow, leaving a tiny mark there for all to see, and vanished in the morning light.

The nurse found the babe sleeping soundly well into the day. He was wrapped in a cloth of stranger's weave. His thumb was in his mouth, along with a piece of the shawl. She did not know how the cloth got there, nor did his grandfather, the Great MacLeod. If his grandmother guessed, she did not say.

But the young laird Jamie knew. He knew that Aizel had been drawn back across the bridge by her son's crying, as surely as he had first been led to her by the barking of his hound.

"Love calls to love," he whispered softly to his infant son as he held him close. "And the fey, like the MacLeods, take care of their own."

The faery shawl still hangs on the wall at Dunvegan Castle on the Isle of Skye. Only now it is called a Faery Flag, and the MacLeods carry it foremost into battle. I have seen it there. Like this story, it is a tattered remnant of stranger's weave and as true and warming as you let it be. ✒️

Dreams Within Dreams

I have gone out and seen the lands of Faery,
　　And have found sorrow and peace and beauty there,
And have not known one from the other, but found each
　　Lovely and gracious alike, delicate and fair.

"They are children of one mother, she that is called Longing,
　　Desire, Love," one told me: and another, "Her secret name
Is Wisdom": and another, "They are not three but one":
　　And another, "Touch them not, seek them not, they are wind
　　　and flame."

I have come back from the hidden, silent lands of Faery
　　And have forgotten the music of its ancient streams:
And now flame and wind and the long, grey, wandering wave
　　And beauty and peace and sorrow are dreams within dreams.

FIONA MACLEOD

The Three Fairies of Sandy Batoum

GREECE

 HERE WAS ONCE A BOY who was apprenticed to a butcher just at the time the king's daughter was to be wed.

The king came to the butcher and said, "You owe me much, and to settle part of that debt, I want forty sheep for my daughter's wedding tomorrow and all of them still warm." Then he left, slamming the door behind.

The butcher put his head in his hands. "How can I do such a thing?" he cried.

But the boy laughed. "Can there be anything easier? Just bring me a bag of nuts and come back in the morning."

So the butcher put his fate in the boy's hand and left.

THE BOY SAT up all night, eating the nuts. At dawn he prayed to God, and God heard him and sent the forty sheep, ready for eating, and they were still warm.

The butcher was so pleased that, after the king's daughter's wedding, he told the boy, "You shall be my son and marry my daughter." He neglected to say that the girl was already betrothed to another. The butcher was not a very smart man.

Well, the girl's fiancé was not pleased and determined to rid himself of his rival. So he took the boy to a strange meadow, saying, "Let us make a party here, to show there are no bad feelings between us."

The boy liked the sound of that.

"Do you see that vine over there?" the fiancé said. "It has grapes both winter and summer. Go and bring some for us to eat."

Now that vine was thought to grow in a vile place. It was said that wicked fairies lived thereabouts. Whoever climbed the vine never returned.

But the boy did not know this. He went to the vine, said a prayer to God, and was about to climb up when he heard a noise behind him. Turning, he saw a fairy maiden, as lovely as spring.

He grabbed her by the hair and threw her to the ground, whereupon she turned into a dove with great white wings and a golden beak.

"Take this golden bracelet," said the dove. "And if you search for me, you will find me in Sandy Batoum." Then she flew off.

The boy took the bracelet and some grapes as well, but when he returned to the table, the fiancé had run off, so the boy went home alone.

WELL, THAT VERY NEXT day, having seen his daughter and her new husband off on a trip, the king came to the butcher once again.

"You must now bring the rest of what you owe me," said the king. "And by my accounting it is three hundred and fifty gold pieces." He left, slamming the door behind.

The butcher put his head in his hands. "How can I do such a thing?" he cried.

The boy laughed. "Can there be anything easier? Take this bracelet and sell it and pay your debt."

So the butcher went to the market and found a gold merchant who said, "Where did you find this? It is mine. I shall have you arrested." He called for the authorities and immediately the butcher was taken to court.

But the boy went to speak on his behalf, saying, "It is my fault, not the butcher's. However, if you give me forty days, I will go and fetch another bracelet just like it so you can see that it is not the merchant's but mine."

So the boy was given his forty days, but the butcher remained in jail the while.

The first thing the boy did was to ask around about fairies. And, hearing that there were dangerous fairies on the sea sinking all boats in a certain sea-lane, he borrowed a boat and rowed out to sea. There, in the very middle of the sea-lane, was a fairy as beautiful as summer. She had been seizing the rudder of each boat that passed and sinking every one.

The boy stood up and grabbed her by the hair and dashed her to the plankings of his little boat. She turned into a dove just like the other fairy, with great white wings and a golden beak. And like the other, she, too, said, "Take this golden bracelet. And if you search for me, you will find me in Sandy Batoum." Then she flew off.

·   ·   ·

THE BOY WENT back to shore, but when he landed he saw that the city was draped in black mourning cloth.

"Who has died?" he asked an old woman.

"The king's son," she answered. "He had a stroke and died at once. He has been placed in his tomb."

"Show me the tomb, then," said the boy.

So the old woman brought him to the place where the prince had been buried, with a white marble marker over the site, gleaming in the bright sun. The boy dug a hole under the tomb, and there he saw the king's son being tickled and tickled by a fairy, and she was as beautiful as the year round.

The boy reached down and grabbed a handful of her hair and pulled her up to the surface of the earth where he threw her on the ground. She, too, turned into a dove just like the other fairies, with great white wings and a golden beak. And, like the others, she, too, said, "Take this golden bracelet. And if you search for me, you will find me in Sandy Batoum." Then off she flew.

The boy reached back down under the marble marker and drew the king's son up by the hair, and the prince was alive. So the boy took him at once to his father, the king.

The king was puzzled and overjoyed at the same time, but the boy said nothing about the fairy. And neither did the prince, though whether it was because he did not remember or because he was embarrassed, I cannot say.

"Ask of me what you will, " said the king to the butcher's boy.

"Find me a man to take me to Sandy Batoum," said the boy.

SO AN OLD MAN was found who knew the way to everywhere in the world, and he led the boy by the hand over three mountains and through three valleys.

When at last they were beyond anywhere the boy or the butcher or the king had ever known, the old man stopped and pointed ahead. "I will go no farther," the man said. "From here you must go alone."

"That I shall," said the boy, "if it pleases God."

"Well said," replied the man. "Now listen carefully. Ahead you will find the house of the three fairies of Sandy Batoum. Take three sheep with you for there are three lions guarding the gates. Give a sheep to each lion, and you will be allowed to pass through. This I have on good authority, though I have never been there myself."

So the boy did as the old man directed, giving one sheep to each lion, and when he got to the fairies' house, he hid himself behind a door and watched.

Soon three doves flew in through the window, and when they touched the floor they turned into the three fairies, the one as lovely as spring, the second as lovely as summer, and the third as lovely as the year round.

They sat down at a table, and it was magically laid for them, with bread and cheese and wine as red as blood.

"Tell me, sisters," said the eldest, "what have you been doing? For the following happened to me. I was standing beneath a vine, guarding the grapes of long life, when a young man grabbed my hair and threw me to the

ground," She held up her glass. "That he could see me and that he could rule me, I drink his health." And she drank the glass down to the dregs.

The middle sister said, "Well, I was sinking boats in the sea-lanes that they not go off to war, and a young man came by and grabbed me by the hair and dashed me to the deck. And that he could see me and could rule me, I drink his health." And she, too, drank her wine.

Then the youngest said, "I was under the royal tomb tickling the king's son, who had fallen into a faint and had been buried while still alive, and a young man dragged me out by the hair and flung me to the earth. And that he could see me and could rule me, I drink his health."

But before the youngest could drink her wine, the butcher's boy came from behind the door. "I am that young man," he said, and showed them the two golden bracelets on his arm.

Then the three fairies leaped up and came over to him and covered him with kisses, asking, "Why have you come here? To get more golden bracelets?"

"One more from you," he said to the eldest fairy. "And one more from you," he said to the middle fairy. But he asked none of the youngest, who was as lovely as the year round.

So they gave him the bracelets and now he had four—one for the butcher and three for himself. Then the fairies gave him his choice of mount. One lion could carry him back home in three hours, the second in two hours, and the third in half an hour.

He mounted the third lion and got to the marketplace where the merchant was still selling his wares.

The boy summoned the members of the law court to watch. He put the four bracelets down on the merchant's table and the law court put down the fifth.

"Which one is yours?" asked the boy.

The merchant shook his head. "They are all the same."

So the butcher was let out of jail and used his bracelet to pay off the king. The merchant was sent packing.

As for the boy…well, the boy mounted the lion once again and in half an hour was back at the fairies' home. He married the youngest fairy, the one as lovely as the year round, ate of the grapes of long life, and lived happily ever after. ✐❦

The Fountain of the Fairies

There is a fountain in the forest call'd
The Fountain of the Fairies: when a child
With a delightful wonder I have heard
Tales of the elfin tribe who on its banks
Hold midnight revelry. An ancient oak,
The goodliest of the forest, grows beside;
Alone it stands, upon a green grass plat,
By the woods bounded like some little isle.
It ever hath been deem'd their favourite tree,
They love to lie and rock upon its leaves,
And bask in moonshine. Here the woodman leads
His boy, and showing him the green-sward mark'd
With darker circlets, says the midnight dance
Hath traced the rings, and bids him spare the tree.
Fancy had cast a spell upon the place
Which made it holy; and the villagers
Would say that never evil thing approach'd
Unpunish'd there. The strange and fearful pleasure
Which fill'd me by that solitary spring,
Ceased not in riper years; and now it wakes
Deeper delight, and more mysterious awe.

ROBERT SOUTHEY

The Stolen Wife

NEW ZEALAND — MAORI

IN THE LONG AGO, THERE LIVED a fisherman named Ruarangi who had a wife so beautiful, even the fairies were jealous of her. They talked about her incessantly, their voices sounding to the humans like bellbirds in the trees.

The fairy king, hearing from his people about this lovely woman, decided to see her for himself. As he was invisible in the daylight, he flew to her home and watched her as she walked in her garden.

Even fairies can fall in love. He felt such a longing for the beautiful woman that he could barely eat or drink.

"I will wait till Ruarangi is off on a fishing voyage," he said to his people, "and then I will take her."

"Will you take her while she sleeps?" asked his fairy adviser.

The king shook his head, for to take a sleeping human meant that only the soul was carried away and that the human's body dies. He did not want that. He wanted the woman body *and* soul.

"I will take her when she is awake," he said. And though it was not often done this way, it was what the king wished.

So the very next time Ruarangi sailed off, the fairy king went to his house and hovered outside the door, calling in a voice like a tui—that musical forest bird—now soft, now loud, now enticing.

Ruarangi's wife left the fire and came outside and walked to her garden to search for the calling bird, for such singing brought tears to her eyes.

The fairy king swooped down and enfolded her in his wings, then lifted her up and up, higher and higher, till the world was lost to her. Then, still singing in her ear, a voice that made her forget all that she had known, the king carried her to his own house and garden.

"Now you are truly home," he sang to her. And so she believed.

It was not a hard life, for the love of fairies is infinitely gentle and kind. She never thought of her mortal husband, but listened to the fairy singing, the pipings of the king's flautist, and to the love words of the king himself.

WHEN RUARANGI RETURNED from his fishing voyage, he discovered that his wife was gone. Distracted, he ran through the garden and down the path. He searched the woods and pools nearby. But she was not to be found.

The other villagers helped in his search, and for days they looked everywhere, calling her name in loud voices till all of them were hoarse.

At last Ruarangi went to the *tohunga*, the village priest who was well-versed in magic and had knowledge of unseen things.

"Please," cried Ruarangi, "please help me find my beloved wife."

The *tohunga* replied, "I will do what I can," for he had known Ruarangi as a boy and was fond of him. He called up a Seeking spell and discovered that Ruarangi's wife had been taken both body and soul by the fairy king.

"Then I shall never see her again," Ruarangi cried, putting his head in his hands.

"*Never* is a word that is too big for me to understand," said the *tohunga*. "What is it your wife loves to do most of all?"

Ruarangi thought and thought. "She will always stop to listen to the birds," he said. "She knows them each by their songs."

The *tohunga* smiled. "Then she will know this one best of all." And he began a *karakia*, an incantation. From his incantation there came the trilling song of the *ngiru-ngiru*, the Maori lovebird.

That song traveled from the village, through the woods, across one mountain and then another and then another after that till it came at last to the palace of the fairy king. The song fluttered like the lovebird itself and landed on a branch in the fairy king's garden. There, walking through the fairy grove, where strange and wonderful fruit hung down from the trees all year round, was Ruarangi's wife.

She had been a full year entranced by the fairy singing. She had been a full year transfixed by their unearthly songs. But when the lovebird's little call sang from the branch of a tree, she stopped. *That* was something new. And something old. Something she thought she remembered.

With that memory, small and compact as the lovebird itself, came another. A face and a laugh.

It was the memory of her husband in the world.

Ruarangi.

Suddenly she longed for him, her husband, and it was a pang under the breast, like a sharp thorn that was both painful and wonderful at the same time.

"Ruarangi," she whispered.

"Ruarangi!" she said aloud. At her voice, the fairy king's spell was broken in two.

She looked around, wondering where she was. Then she walked

through the fairy grove and through a gate in the wall surrounding it. There in the distance was her husband, Ruarangi, who had traveled from the village, through the woods, across one mountain and then another, and then another after that, to come at last to the palace of the fairy king.

"Ruarangi!" she cried, and he ran to her.

Then he enfolded a cloth around her shoulders and led her back into the world. She looked pale and cold. A year with the fairies will do that to any mortal. But he brought her into their house and cooked food for her and fed it to her with his own hand. After a while, the color returned to her face, and she smiled at him, which had a warmth of its very own.

MEANWHILE THE FAIRY KING, furious to find the human woman gone, flew after them, across one mountain, then another and another, through the woods and into the village. He arrived at Ruarangi's house in the daylight, and so he was invisible.

But the *tohunga* was there, outside, waiting. What was invisible to others was visible to him. He saw the fairy king in all his power and beauty.

So the *tohunga* sang out an incantation, the most powerful he had ever tried. He sang of the love of one human for another, of the children yet to be born between this man and this woman. He sang of the joy of hard work and the soft rest after—all things that the fairies knew not.

The fairy king was caught by the *tohunga*'s enchantment and was unable to come into Ruarangi's house. And by the end of the priest's *karakia*, the fairy king had forgotten Ruarangi's wife altogether and returned to his own palace, alone. 🌱

The Fairy Musicians

The treble was a three-mouthed grasshopper,
Well-tutored by a skilful chorister:
An ancient master, that did use to play
The friskings which the lambs do dance in May.
And long time was the chiefest called to sing,
When on the plains the fairies made a ring;
Then a field-cricket, with a note full clean,
Sweet and unforced and softly sung the mean,
To whose accord, and with no mickle labour,
A pretty fairy played upon a tabor:
The case was of a hazel-nut, the heads
A bat's wing dressed, the snares were silver threads;
A little stiffened lamprey's skin did suit
All the rest well, and served them for a flute;
And to all these a deep well-breasted gnat,
That had good sides, knew well his sharp and flat,
Sung a good compass, making no wry face, —
Was there as fittest for a chamber-bass.
    These choice musicians to their merry king
Gave all the pleasures which their art could bring.

WILLIAM BROWNE

Flower Fairies

Flower fairies—have you found them,
　　When the summer's dusk is falling,
With the glow-worms watching round them;
　　Have you heard them softly calling?

Silent stand they through the noonlight,
　　In their flower shapes, fair and quiet;
But they hie them forth by moonlight
　　Ready then to sing and riot.

I have heard them; I have seen them,—
　　Light from their bright petals raying;
And the trees bent down to screen them,
　　Great, wise trees, too old for playing.

Hundreds of them, all together,—
　　Flashing flocks of flying fairies,
Crowding through the summer weather,
　　Seeking where the coolest air is.

And they tell the trees that know them,
　　As upon their boughs they hover,
Of the things that chance below them,—
　　How the rose has a new lover.

And the gay Rose laughs, protesting,
    "Neighbour Lily is as fickle."
Then they search where birds are nesting,
    And their feathers softly tickle.

Then away they all dance, sweeping,
    Having drunk their fill of gladness.
But the trees, their night-watch keeping,
    Thrill with tender, pitying sadness;

For they know of bleak December,
    When each bough left cold and bare is,—
When they only shall remember
    The bright visits of the fairies,—

When the roses and the lilies
    Shall be gone, to come back never
From the land where all so still is
    That they sleep and sleep for ever.

PHILIP BOURKE MARSTON

The Tailor's Treasure

I N OLD BRITTANY, WHERE THE FAIRIES of the land are called Margot-la-Fee, a tailor did a favor for a rich fairy lady. In return she gave him the key to her cavern, which had been scooped out of the rocks as a rough shelter from the rains.

"Take what you will," said the Margot-la-Fee. "Or take what you can." She smiled, and her green eyes looked like the sun through trees.

So the tailor took the key, but he forgot to thank her, which was a very silly thing to do. He hurried to the cavern, opened the door, and went in.

What should he discover there but three enormous piles of money. The first pile—all gold coins called *louis d'or*—sat atop a white sheep. The second pile—all silver coins—rested on the back of a gray sheep. The third pile—all copper coins—lay across the back of a black sheep.

"And who gave you permission to enter?" asked the white sheep, blinking her strange green eyes.

"My lady Margot-la-Fee," said the tailor. He held up the key. "She told me to take what I will or what I can."

"Then take it will ye, nil ye," said the white sheep.

The other sheep nodded, but said nothing.

So the tailor put the key in his mouth and filled his pockets with coins—gold, silver, and copper. But there was plenty left he could not carry.

"Would you be able to carry even more," said the sheep at last, "if you went back and fetched a sack?"

The tailor struck his hand to his head. "Of course!" he mumbled, spitting out the key. He emptied his pockets and shook out his shirt and ran from the cavern all the way home.

In less than an hour he was back with the largest sack he could find. But search as hard as he could, and as long as he might, he could not find the Margot's cave again. ✑

Where to Find Fairies

Up and down the mossy glens,
Through the greeny bowers,
Hiding under inky caps,
Safe from evening showers;

Dancing through the hedgerows,
Napping in an oak,
Singing through the fresh rye grass—
That's where you'll find the Folk.

JANE YOLEN

Three Short Welsh Fairy Stories

WALES

HERE WAS A FARMER AND HIS WIFE in Blaen Pennant in Wales, and they had one son, who was a handsome youth and a hard worker, named David.

David wooed and wed a fairy, one of the *Tylwyth Teg*, who said to him that they would long be happy if there was no iron in the house nor lock on the door.

So it was done, and no couple lived happier.

But one day they had a horse that would not be bridled, and in his anger, the farmer's son threw the bridle at the obstreperous stallion.

The bridle missed the horse and hit the wife. And no sooner had the bit touched her than she disappeared, carrying away all happiness with her.

A fairy, one of the *Tylwyth Teg,* was in the habit of helping a family in the Pennant Valley every evening by putting the children to bed. She would sing them fairy songs until they were fast asleep.

Poor fairy, she was ill clad in rags, and the mistress of the house felt sorry for her. So one night she gave the fairy a silken gown to thank her for all the help.

But fairies do not like rewards. The very next day the fairy was gone, and the gown was found at the foot of the dairy, torn all to shreds.

Once there was a man who lived in a small cottage by the side of a mountain. There he tilled a little garden with good cheer.

One day he noticed a rook's nest in the tree overlooking his potato plot, and it struck him that it might be prudent to break up the nest before the rooks multiplied.

So he climbed up and broke the nest, and, as he came back down the tree, he saw that there was a fairy ring around the tree. And in the circle he spied a golden coin.

The next morning, out hoeing weeds from his garden, he saw yet another coin under the tree.

So it went day after day. *Soon I will be rich.* he thought. And he told a friend, taking him to the very spot of his fortune.

But the next day there was no gold coin waiting him, for he had broken the first rule of the fairy folk—that their gifts must never be mentioned.

The Lost Spear

ONCE THERE WAS A GREAT KING whose daughter, Unanana, was of marriageable age. So to be certain that her suitors were the finest hunters in the land, he declared a contest for her hand.

"Whoever is the strongest and can throw my royal spear—the *assegai*—the farthest will be my son-in-law."

Now many chiefs gathered for the contest and with them their sons and their sons' sons. Not only were the king's lands of interest to them, but Unanana herself was known to be a great beauty.

Three days and three nights, the men feasted and engaged in mock combat, until at last there were four who were clearly the strongest.

"These four," declared the great king, "will throw the *assegai*."

Now three of the chosen were the sons of chieftains, but the fourth was a handsome lad named Zandilli, and he was but a poor herdsman. Yet Princess Unanana had eyes only for him.

The great king had the four stand in a row on a sandy plain. Then he handed the *assegai* to the first young man.

This one was the oldest son of a famous warrior. He stood tall and proud. When he threw the spear, it flew quickly through the air and landed upright in an anthill on the edge of sight.

"Ha!" cried the king. "You are surely the strongest. My daughter is all but yours."

But when the second young man got ready to throw, he was even taller and prouder than the first, for he was the son of a famous hunter. His throw flew even more quickly through the air and went past the anthill and pierced the heart of an ironwood tree.

"Ha!" cried the king. "You are surely the strongest. My daughter is all but yours."

Then the third young man got ready to throw, and he was even taller and prouder than the first two, for his father was famous as both a hunter and a warrior. His throw surpassed the others and hit a hawk in flight that carried the *assegai* farther still.

"Ha!" cried the king. "I see that you are the strongest of the three. My daughter is surely yours."

The herdsman now came forward and when the *assegai* was returned, he held out his hand.

The king made a face. He thought no one could better that third throw, and besides, he did not want the herdsman to marry his daughter.

The herdsman bowed to the king, and turned and smiled at Unanana. Then he turned back and threw the *assegai*. Like lightning the *assegai* flew, past the anthill, past the ironwood tree, past the place where the dead hawk lay, and out of sight.

Loud were the cries of praise from all of the people, but loudest still was the voice of Unanana. "Zandilli is the strongest of them all!"

But the great king was not pleased. "Tomorrow there will be another contest," he said. "And all will throw with spears of gold."

In the morning the four men threw. The three were given spears that were perfectly balanced, but the herdsman was given a clumsy spear, unbalanced and untrue.

Yet again the herdsman's *assegai* flew farther than the others, into the very clouds, where it was lost from sight.

"I claim Princess Unanana as my bride," said Zandilli. "For I have proved that I am the strongest."

"Not until you bring me back the golden spear and lay it here at my feet," said the king.

Unanana flung herself at her father's feet. "You are unjust, Father," she cried. "Zandilli has won the contest not once but twice."

"Nevertheless, I have spoken," said the king.

Princess Unanana stood and put her hands on her hips. "I will remind you what the wise men say: *A word uttered cannot be taken back.* When Zandilli returns with the spear, we will be married."

So Zandilli went at once to seek the lost golden spear, wandering for days among the mountains.

On the fourth day, as he gazed into a brown pool wondering where to go next, a butcher-bird fell at his feet, a little green frog clutched in its talons.

"Help me!" cried the frog.

Zandilli grabbed up the butcher-bird and freed the frog from its grip, then he flung the bird back up into the sky.

The frog blinked its golden eyes. "If ever you are in trouble, man, think of this brown pond, and I will come to help."

"How can you help me?" asked Zandilli. "With all my strength, I cannot do what must be done. And you are so small."

The frog chuggered. "Do not the wise men say, 'Even an ant can help an elephant'?" And it hopped into the pond and was gone.

Zandilli went on and found a large yellow and black butterfly impaled upon the thorns of a tree.

"Help me!" cried the butterfly.

Carefully Zandilli pulled the butterfly free.

"If ever you are in trouble, man, think of this thorn tree, and I will come to help."

"How can you help me?" asked Zandilli. "With all my strength, I cannot do what must be done. And you are so small."

The butterfly flapped its wings. "Do not the wise men say, 'Even an ant can help an elephant'?" Then it flapped twice and was gone.

NIGHT WAS DARKENING the sky of the fifth day, and still Zandilli had not found the king's spear. Eager to find shelter, Zandilli stumbled into a wild gorge and came upon a small cave.

Zandilli entered the cave and lay down to rest. No sooner had he done so than he heard sweet music coming from farther in. As Zandilli knew no fear, he stood and wound his way through the blackness toward that unearthly music.

The music grew louder with every step, and at last a faint light appeared ahead of him.

Astonished, Zandilli kept going forward until at last he found himself at an underground lake lit by an eerie light. The cave mounded high like a dome over the lake and shone with the glitter of a thousand bright stones.

In the very center of the lake were golden steps leading to a throne on which sat the most beautiful woman Zandilli had ever seen. She had feathery wings and white hair that curled down to her waist.

Then, floating on large rose-colored lilies, came a hundred other fairies, their wings translucent and fine. They gathered before the throne, and Zandilli realized they were the source of the music.

He could not move for fear of frightening them all away.

But suddenly the fairy on the throne spoke. "Mortal," she said, "we, the Moon Fairies, have been waiting for you. We know what it is you seek."

Zandilli flung himself down on the stone floor crying, "Oh, Mighty Being, help me find the spear that I may wed the beautiful Unanana."

"We can give you only what you can win," the fairy queen said. "For it was prophesied at the beginning of time that a mortal would come to our hidden home and ask for something in our possession which we could give him only if he performed two tasks for us."

"Ask and I shall do them," cried Zandilli.

The queen came down the golden steps and got onto one of the lily boats. She came to the shore and gestured to Zandilli, who climbed aboard.

Then, with the rest of the Moon Fairies following, they floated through the tunnels of the cave.

Wonder after bright wonder unfolded before them, but there was one dark cavern that seemed a blot upon the fairies' home.

"There," said the queen. "If, before the moon rises again, you can make *that* cavern as beautiful as the others, you will have performed your first task. Fail—and you shall die."

Zandilli was left in a golden canoe at the gaping door of the black cavern and the fairies sailed away.

"What have I done?" he asked himself. "There is no way I can make beautiful this dark place in so short a time. I shall die in the morning." He thought about all that he would be leaving behind: the beautiful Unanana, the towering mountains, the gold-flecked waters, his own small flock, the birds, the butterflies...

Zandilli laughed. He remembered the butterfly he had saved from the thorn tree. "If ever you could help me," he said aloud, "help me now."

There was a sudden shiver in the air, as if a thousand thousand small wings were fluttering toward him. Zandilli shivered, closed his eyes, and slept.

When he opened them again, the black cavern had been transformed into a fairy palace by the gorgeous wings of butterflies and fireflies who spread themselves out across the cavern walls.

The fairy queen and her followers arrived on their lily boats. With one voice, they cried, "He has done it! He has done it!" And the fairy queen smiled.

BUT THERE WAS still the second task.

"Here is the golden spear you seek," said the fairy queen. "I will place it on the steps of my throne so you can see we do not promise what we cannot give."

"I see it, my queen," said Zandilli.

"Your second task is this: My fairy maidens' wings are woven from the wings of flies. But alas, we have no more. Our looms stand idle, our storerooms empty. Fill those storerooms by tomorrow morning, else you shall die."

Zandilli nodded, but in his heart he felt only despair. The first task had been difficult enough. But the second was beyond doing.

Oh little frog in the brown pond, he thought, *if you could only help me as the butterfly did*. Then he fell asleep, dreaming of all he was about to lose.

But the little frog heard his call and gathered all its kin and its lizard cousins as well. Each came to the cavern with a bundle of flies and left them in the storeroom. Hundreds of flies. Thousands of flies. Perhaps even millions of flies.

When the queen and her followers came the next morning, they cried, "He has done it! He has done it!"

The queen smiled and handed Zandilli the golden spear. "Go, mortal, and know that it was your tender heart that won you your spear. Strength is nothing without the heart. Remember that when you are wed."

Zandilli bowed his head. "I will remember," he said.

And he did. ✒

The Ruin

When the last colours of the day
Have from their burning ebbed away,
About that ruin, cold and lone,
The cricket shrills from stone to stone;
And scattering o'er its darkened green,
Bands of the fairies may be seen,
Chattering like grasshoppers, their feet
Dancing a thistledown dance round it:
While the great gold of the mild moon
Tinges their tiny acorn shoon.

WALTER DE LA MARE

Angus Mor and the Fairies

 N Inverness, not far from Loch Ness, stood a fine farm, and on that farm was a shepherd named Angus Mor. Every day, whether rain or fair, Angus was out with his dog and his sheep.

Now one evening, and a wet, misty, gray evening it was, Angus was just turning for home. As he came around the hill, the sheep ahead of him and the dog at his heel, he heard a voice come out of a rock.

Now a voice from a rock would have been marvel enough. But this voice sounded like Janet Mcdonald, the lass he was to marry that very next day.

He stopped still and listened, wondering where she could be hiding. And wondering further what she was doing on the path when she should be at home preparing for their wedding. Angus was not one to make romances out of rocks. But his sweetheart did not come out to greet him.

So he went around the rock, and what should appear before him but a lovely green hillock with an opening door. And out of that door cascaded a brilliant light that made the hillock look as if it were drenched in day.

Music, too, came out of that door, so sweet that Angus had tears in his eyes.

He crept toward the door, but, in a moment of caution, he thrust his iron knife into the side post of the door, then he peeped in.

There, inside the hillock, was a company of fairy folk in a circle, wheeling and spinning and dancing with such energy, Angus was dizzy just watching.

He didn't move a bit, just listened to the fairy music and kept time with his hand. But when a fairy came out and went to fetch water from a nearby brook, Angus stood up in the path before her.

"Let me by, Angus Mor," said the fairy. She knew his name, of course. Fairies always do.

"Not until you tell me whose voice I heard in the rock," said he.

"I may not tell thee," the fairy replied.

"Then you shall not pass," said he.

"If not with thy goodwill, then I will pass in spite of thee," said the fairy. And she dodged past him.

But Angus had his shepherd's crook, which had an iron spike on one end. He threw the crook at the fairy, and immediately the iron touched her—fairies can't abide cold iron—she fell to the ground. Before she could rise, Angus had hold of her.

"Tell me quick—what woman was calling from that rock?" he said.

"Angus Mor," she answered, "that was the fairy queen. And if you cannot tell the secret of our queen on the bridge of Easan Dubh, a week from tonight, thy wife and son will be ours."

Angus wondered greatly at this, for he had neither wife nor child yet, but as the fairy had no more to tell him, he let her go. Then he went straight home, with his sheep and his dog, and got married in the morning, and thought no more of the warning. Indeed he considered it but a dream.

Now less than a week passed, and Angus Mor was once again on the mountain with his dog and sheep and once again he found himself by the fairy knoll where the light streamed out of the door. Dream or not, he crept close and peered inside. This time there was neither music nor dance, but the same little fairy was on the path with a bucket of water in her hand.

"Angus Mor," she said as she passed him by, "thy wife and son are ours if you cannot tell the secret of our queen by this Friday." And Friday, Angus knew, was but a day away.

ANGUS HURRIED HOME. Once might have been a dream. But twice was a warning.

His new wife, Janet, met him at the door, and she could see by his face that something troubled him.

"Tell me, dearest," she said.

And he did.

"Do not trouble yourself more, Angus," she replied. "For about a year ago I, too, went by the fairy knoll and, feeling faint, sat down to rest. When I awoke, I was inside the knoll, inside the fairy house, and all about me were the fairy folk dancing and whirling and twirling. I tried to leave, for goodness knows we human folk should not mix with the fairies. But each time I tried to go, the fairies blocked my way."

"Did they hurt you?" asked Angus, great concern in his voice.

"No, but one of them, who seemed to be the king of them all, said to me that I could go only if I promised to be his wife unless I could get my chosen love in marriage by the end of one year."

"One year?" asked Angus. "Why did you not tell me?"

"I could not," said Janet. "The fairy king sealed my lips. But as you

were my chosen love, and since we were married before the time set, I am free from my promise to the fairy king."

"But we are not free yet," Angus pointed out. "For surely the queen wishes to hurt you since you had taken the eye of her king."

They talked long into the night and at last came up with a plan.

So on Friday, long long before evening, Angus Mor went to the bridge of Easan Dubh. He and Janet had thought of many secrets between them. A hundred hundred or more. Janet had written them down, and he had the list in a leather bag around his neck.

He sat down on top of the bridge, his good dog at his side. And as he was sitting and thinking of more things to add to the list, he heard a sweet voice singing under the bridge.

Quietly he peeped over the side, and who did he see but the queen of fairies herself, cleaning and rubbing clothes on a stone and singing:

I know Ben More in Mull,
I know the top of Scuir Eigg,
I know the cat that was in Ulva
With its tail turned to the fire.
There is music in the hall of my dear;
There is gold in the land of Mackay,
But there is a song in Inverness
Which shall never be known.

Horin O Ro Hoorio Horo.

Angus leaned over and laughed. "Thou art wrong, oh fairy queen," he called. "I have every word of thy song, thy secret song!"

The fairy queen looked up and cried, "Thy son and wife are now thine forever, Angus Mor." And in a flash she was gone.

In nine months Janet delivered a fine baby boy. And Angus Mor and his family, his sheep, and his dog were never troubled by the fairies again. ✒

Over Hill, Over Dale

Over hill, over dale,
Thorough bush, thorough brier,
Over park, over pale,
Thorough flood, thorough fire:
I do wander everywhere,
Swifter than the moones sphere;
And I serve the fairy queen,
To dew her orbs upon the green.
The cowslips tall her pensioners be;
In their gold coats spots you see;
Those be rubies, fairy favours,
In those freckles live their savours:
I must go seek some dew-drops here,
And hang a pearl in every cowslip's ear.

WILLIAM SHAKESPEARE

Source Notes

THOMAS THE RHYMER: I used the basic ballad in Sir Walter Scott's collection *Minstrelsy of the Scottish Border* (1909) and material from Raymond Lamont-Brown's *Scottish Folklore* (Edinburgh: Birlinn Limited, 1996) as well as research from Katharine Briggs's various wonderful books on fairy mythology: *Abbey Lubbers, Banshees, and Boggarts: An Illustrated Encyclopedia of Fairies* (New York: Pantheon Books, 1979), *The Fairies in English Tradition and Literature* (London: Routledge and Kegan Paul Limited, 1967), and *The Vanishing People: Fairy Lore and Legends* (New York: Pantheon Books, 1978).

THE PERI WIFE comes from an outline of a story in Thomas Keightley's *The Fairy Mythology* (London: George Bell and Sons, 1892).

THE FAIRY MIDWIFE combines several stories from Thomas Keightley's *The Fairy Mythology* (London: George Bell and Sons, 1892) as well as research from Katharine Briggs's books on fairy mythology: *Abbey Lubbers, Banshees, and Boggarts: An Illustrated Encyclopedia of Fairies* (New York: Pantheon Books, 1979), *The Fairies in English Tradition and Literature* (London: Routledge and Kegan Paul Limited, 1967), and *The Vanishing People: Fairy Lore and Legends* (New York: Pantheon Books, 1978).

THE FEE'S CHANGELING is retold from a shorter version in Thomas Keightley's *The Fairy Mythology* (London: George Bell and Sons, 1892) as well as research from Katharine Briggs's books on fairy mythology: *Abbey Lubbers, Banshees, and Boggarts: An Illustrated Encyclopedia of Fairies* (New York: Pantheon Books, 1979), *The Fairies in English Tradition and Literature* (London: Routledge and Kegan Paul Limited, 1967), and *The Vanishing People: Fairy Lore and Legends* (New York: Pantheon Books, 1978).

THE FAIRIES BANISHED is retold from Thomas Keightley's *The Fairy Mythology* (London: George Bell and Sons, 1892) as well as research from Katharine Briggs's books on fairy mythology: *Abbey Lubbers, Banshees, and Boggarts: An Illustrated Encyclopedia of Fairies* (New York: Pantheon Books, 1979), *The Fairies in English Tradition and Literature* (London: Routledge and Kegan Paul Limited, 1967), and *The Vanishing People: Fairy Lore and Legends* (New York: Pantheon Books, 1978).

THE FAERY FLAG was originally published in my own collection *The Faery Flag* (New York: Orchard Books, 1989), and my original research was done at Dunvegan Castle in Scotland.

THE THREE FAIRIES OF SANDY BATOUM is a retelling based on a story in R. M. Dawkins's *More Greek Folktales* (Oxford, England: The Clarendon Press, 1955).

THE STOLEN WIFE comes from a basic outline of a story in Jan Knappert's *Pacific Mythology* (London: Diamond Books, 1995).

THE TAILOR'S TREASURE is retold from W. Branch Johnson's *Folktales of Brittany* (London: Methuen & Co., Ltd., 1927).

THREE SHORT WELSH FAIRY STORIES can be found in drier renditions in John Rhys's hefty *Celtic Folklore: Welsh and Manx*, vol. 1 (Oxford, England: The Clarendon Press, 1901) as well as research from Katharine Briggs's books on fairy mythology: *Abbey Lubbers, Banshees, and Boggarts: An Illustrated Encyclopedia of Fairies* (New York: Pantheon Books, 1979), *The Fairies in English Tradition and Literature* (London: Routledge and Kegan Paul Limited, 1967), and *The Vanishing People: Fairy Lore and Legends* (New York: Pantheon Books, 1978).

THE LOST SPEAR can be found in a longer and stranger and probably very corrupt version in Andrew Lang's *The Golden Fairy Book* (New York: A. L. Burt Company, n.d.).

ANGUS MOR AND THE FAIRIES is a retelling from a retelling of the tale in a delicious old illustrated volume by Elizabeth Grierson, *The Scottish Fairy Book* (London: Fischer Unwin, n.d.), and from some extra material found in Katharine Briggs's books on fairy mythology: *Abbey Lubbers, Banshees, and Boggarts: An Illustrated Encyclopedia of Fairies* (New York: Pantheon Books, 1979), *The Fairies in English Tradition and Literature* (London: Routledge and Kegan Paul Limited, 1967), and *The Vanishing People: Fairy Lore and Legends* (New York: Pantheon Books, 1978).

Bibliography

Andrews, Elizabeth. *Ulster Folklore*. London: Eliot Stock, 1913.

Arrowsmith, Nancy, with George Moorse. *A Field Guide to the Little People*. New York: Hill & Wang, 1977.

Briggs, Katharine. *Abbey Lubbers, Banshees, and Boggarts: An Illustrated Encyclopedia of Fairies*. New York: Pantheon Books, 1979.

———.*The Fairies in English Tradition and Literature*. London: Routledge and Kegan Paul Limited, 1967.

———.*The Vanishing People: Fairy Lore and Legends*. New York: Pantheon Books, 1978.

Climo, Shirley. *Piskies, Spriggans, and Other Magical Beings*. New York: Thomas Y. Crowell, 1981.

Dawkins, R. M. *More Greek Folktales*. Oxford, England: The Clarendon Press, 1955.

Grierson, Elizabeth. *The Scottish Fairy Book*. London: Fischer Unwin, n.d.

Johnson, W. Branch. *Folktales of Brittany*. London: Methuen & Co., Ltd., 1927.

Keightley, Thomas. *The Fairy Mythology*. London: George Bell and Sons, 1892.

Knappert, Jan. *Pacific Mythology*. London: Diamond Books, 1995.

Lamont-Brown, Raymond. *Scottish Folklore*. Edinburgh: Birlinn Limited, 1996.

Lang, Andrew. *The Golden Fairy Book*. New York: A. L. Burt Company, n.d.

MacDougall, Rev. James. *Highland Fairy Legends*. Totowa, New Jersey: Rowman and Littlefield, 1978.

Rhys, John. *Celtic Folklore: Welsh and Manx*, vol. 1. Oxford, England: The Clarendon Press, 1901.

Robertson, R. MacDonald. *Selected Highland Folktales*. London: Oliver & Boyd, 1961.

Scott, Sir Walter. *Minstrelsy of the Scottish Border*, facsimile edition. Edinburgh: Andrew Melrose, 1909.